The Beast in the Bathtub

For a free color catalog describing Gareth Stevens' list of high-quality books, call
1-800-542-2595 (USA) or 1-800-461-9120 (Canada). Gareth Stevens' Fax: (414) 225-0377.

For more stories about the Beast, see
The Beast and the Babysitter
Bully for the Beast!

For Lewis Tyner without whom . . .

Library of Congress Cataloging-in-Publication Data

Stevens, Kathleen.
    The beast in the bathtub.

    Summary: Lewis gets into mischief with an imaginary beast in the bathtub
while his parents are watching television.
    (1. Baths—Fiction. 2. Imagination—Fiction) I. Bowler, Ray, ill. II. Title.
PZ7.S84454Be   1985   (Fic)   85-12691
ISBN 0-918831-15-6 (lib. bdg.)
ISBN 0-8368-1174-7 (trade)

North American edition first published in 1985 by

Gareth Stevens Publishing
1555 North RiverCenter Drive, Suite 201
Milwaukee, Wisconsin 53212, USA

U.S. edition copyright © 1985. Text copyright © 1980 Kathleen
Stevens. Illustrations copyright © 1980 by A. Page-Robertson &
Associates. First published in Australia by Childerset Pty. Ltd.

Printed in the United States of America

9 10 11 12 13 99 98 97 96 95 94

The Beast in the Bathtub

Story by Kathleen Stevens

Illustrated by Ray Bowler

Lewis skidded down the stairs and into the living room.
"I can't take a bath," he announced.
"There's a Beast in the bathtub."

His mom and dad looked up from the television. "Lewis,
you have twenty minutes to get into bed
with the lights out," his mom said. "I don't
care what's in the bathtub. You get upstairs and
take a bath this instant."

"All right," said Lewis, "but you'll be sorry if
the Beast eats me."

He went back upstairs and into the bathroom. He stared at the enormous green Beast that sat in the tub. "Move over, Beast," he said. "My mom says I have to take a bath."

It was a tight fit, but Lewis squeezed between the Beast's front claws, and the Beast propped his scaly jaw on Lewis' head. The only problem then was that Lewis couldn't reach the back of his neck.

"Beast," said Lewis, "would you scrub my neck? And while you're at it, please check behind my ears."

The Beast used lots of soap for lather. Then he filled his mouth with water and squirted it between his teeth to rinse off Lewis.

"Hey! That tickles!" Lewis cried as water ran down his back. The Beast kept squirting, and Lewis began to wriggle. Water sloshed over the side of the tub on to the floor.

Lewis jumped out, filled a glass with cold water, and tossed it at the Beast. "Got you!" he said.

The Beast grinned a toothy grin and slapped his tail. Water sprayed the walls, the sink, the floor – and Lewis.

"Not fair!" Lewis cried. "I just evened things up."

"Lewis!" his father called. "What's going on up there?"

"Oh-oh," Lewis said to the Beast. He stuck his head out of the bathroom door. "I spilled some water," he called. "But don't worry, I'm wiping it up."

Lewis and the Beast mopped the floor with towels. Then Lewis put on his cowboy pajamas and brushed his teeth. The Beast didn't wear pajamas. He didn't brush his teeth either. It's not bad being a beast, Lewis thought.

"Let's get a snack," he suggested.

His mom and dad were still watching television. Lewis pretended he and the Beast were cattle rustlers, trying to sneak by the sheriff and his deputy. They edged past the living room door to the kitchen, and Lewis made off with two apples.

"Easy, old pal," he whispered to the Beast as they tip-toed back upstairs. The sheriff and the deputy didn't hear a thing.

Lewis ate his apple and tossed the core into the waste-paper basket. The Beast ate his apple, core and all.

"Come on, Beast," Lewis said. "Let's have a pillow fight."

He grabbed one pillow off his bed and hit the Beast with it. The Beast flipped the other pillow and hit Lewis on the head . . . The two pillows flew back and forth.

Crash! The Beast missed Lewis and hit a can of marbles instead. The marbles bounced to the floor and rolled in every direction.

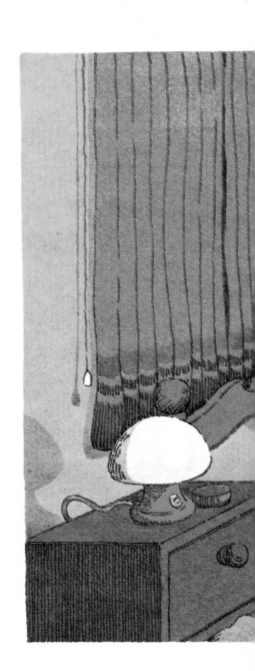

"For heaven's sake, Lewis!" It was his mom calling this time. "What's going on?"

"The marbles fell over," Lewis answered, "but I'm picking them up."

"Hurry up then, and get into bed. Daddy and I will be up in five minutes to kiss you good night."

The Beast swept the marbles together with his forked tail while Lewis picked them up.

"That's it," Lewis said. "We've got them all." He put the can back on the shelf, then knelt down by the bed to say his prayers.

"God bless Mom. God bless Dad. God bless Grandpa and Grandma." Lewis peeked through his laced fingers. The Beast was watching him. "And please, God," Lewis added, "bless the Beast."

The Beast rubbed his scaly jaw on Lewis' shoulder. Lewis offered to share his bed, but the Beast had other plans. He crawled into the darkness under Lewis' bed. Lewis pulled the blanket up to his chin and waited.

Soon he heard his parents on the stairs.

"How nice to find you ready!" his mom said.

She turned off the bedside lamp, while his dad turned on the night light. Then they both kissed him good night.

"Mm-mm," said his mom, "you smell all clean from your bath, Lewis."

"So there isn't a Beast in our bathtub, after all?"
asked his dad, rumpling Lewis' hair.

"Of course not," Lewis replied.

"Well, that's a relief. Good night, Son."

"Sleep well, Lewis," added his mother.

Lewis listened as their footsteps echoed down the hallway. He waited until they went down the stairs.

"Of course there's no Beast in the bathtub," he called. "He's under my bed."